Dear Dragon Eats Out

by Margaret Hillert
Illustrated by David Schimmell

NORWOOD HOUSE PRESS

DEAR CAREGIVER, The *Beginning-to-Read* series is a carefully written collection of classic readers you may remember from your own childhood. Each book features text comprised of common sight words to provide your child ample practice reading the words that appear most frequently in written text. The many additional details in the pictures enhance the story and offer the opportunity for you to help your child expand oral language and develop comprehension.

Begin by reading the story to your child, followed by letting him or her read familiar words and soon your child will be able to read the story independently. At each step of the way, be sure to praise your reader's efforts to build his or her confidence as an independent reader. Discuss the pictures and encourage your child to make connections between the story and his or her own life. At the end of the story, you will find reading activities and a word list that will help your child practice and strengthen beginning reading skills.

Above all, the most important part of the reading experience is to have fun and enjoy it!

Shannon Cannon

Shannon Cannon, Ph.D.
Literacy Consultant

Norwood House Press • P.O. Box 316598 • Chicago, Illinois 60631
For more information about Norwood House Press please visit our website at
www.norwoodhousepress.com or call 866-565-2900.

LIBRARY OF CONGRESS CATALOGING-IN-PUBLICATION DATA
  Hillert, Margaret.
    Dear dragon eats out / by Margaret Hillert ; illustrated by David Schimmell.
      pages cm. -- (A beginning-to-read book)
    Summary: "A boy and his pet dragon go out to eat with Mother. Together they enjoy various breakfast foods and learn about each others favorite foods.This title includes reading activities and a word list"-- Provided by publisher.
    ISBN 978-1-59953-629-3 (library edition : alk. paper) -- ISBN 978-1-60357-638-3 (ebook)
  [1. Food--Fiction. 2. Breakfasts--Fiction. 3. Dragons--Fiction.] I. Schimmell, David, illustrator. II. Title.
    PZ7.H558Dd 2014
    [E]--dc23
                                2013029769

252N–072014
Manufactured in the United States of America in Stevens Point, Wisconsin.

Get up. Get up. Get ready.
Today we are going out to eat.

OK, I will get ready.
I will do this.

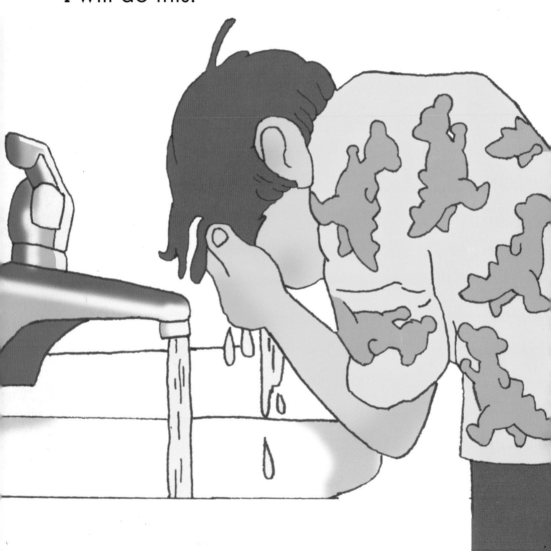

And I will do this.

Here I am Mother.
How do I look?

You look good.
Now let's go!

Come in. Come in.
I have a good spot for you.

Sit down.
Sit down.

Let me help, Mother.
I can do this.

No, No.
I am too big.

Let me sit here.
You sit there.

Put this on.

You will need it.

BREAKFAST MENU

CEREAL
$1.50

JUICE
$1.50

OATMEAL
$1.50

EGGS AND BACON
$3.50

PANCAKES $3.00

MUFFINS $3.50

We have to pick things out to eat.

Oh, boy.
Can I have what I want?

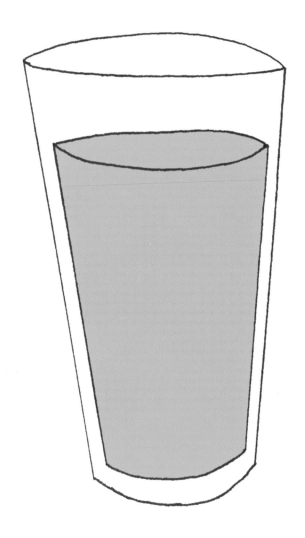

I like orange juice.

I like bacon and eggs.

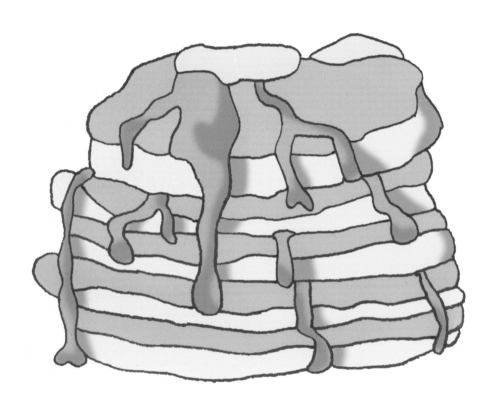

But, I think I'll have these.

Mother, what are you going to eat?

Mother will have eggs.
Dragon and I will have pancakes!

Here it comes.
Here comes something to eat.

Oh, Boy.
This is good.

I am here with you.
And you are here with me.
It is fun to eat out, Dear Dragon!

The following activities support the findings of the National Reading Panel that determined the most effective components for reading instruction are: Phonemic Awareness, Phonics, Vocabulary, Fluency, and Text Comprehension.

Phonemic Awareness: The long e sound

Oddity Task: Say the long **e** (as in Eat) sound for your child. Ask your child to find and say any word that has the long **e** sound in the following word groups:

need, no, next	man, mean, mom	dear, dirt, dart
fun, fan, funny	red, read, road	hip, hop, happy
eat, egg, enjoy	salt, seal, sent	

Phonics: The letter Ee

1. Demonstrate how to form the letters **E** and **e** for your child.

2. Have your child practice writing **E** and **e** at least three times each.

3. Ask your child to point to the words in the book that have the letter **e** in them.

4. Write the words listed below on separate pieces of paper. Read each word aloud and ask your child to repeat them.

dear	happy	ready	family	baby
three	eat	pretty	read	meet
sleep	seat	silly	need	wear

5. Write the following long **e** spellings at the top of a piece of paper.

   ee   ea   y

6. Ask your child to sort the words by placing them under the correct long **e** spelling.

Vocabulary: Naming Objects

1. Ask your child to tell you different words he or she thinks of that go with eating out. Write the words on sticky notes and have the child place them next to any objects he or she has named that are in the story.

2. Ask your child to tell a story using all of the words he or she has come up with that relate to eating out.

Fluency: Echo Reading

1. Reread the story to your child at least two more times while your child tracks the print by running a finger under the words as they are read. Ask your child to read the words he or she knows with you.

2. Reread the story, stopping after each sentence or page to allow your child to read (echo) what you have read. Repeat echo reading and let your child take the lead.

Text Comprehension: Discussion Time

1. Ask your child to retell the sequence of events in the story.

2. To check comprehension, ask your child the following questions:

   • What did Dear Dragon have for breakfast?

   • Why do you think Mother made the boy put the napkin on his shirt?

   • When you get up in the morning what are some things you do to get ready for the day?

   • What are some of your favorite foods to eat?

WORD LIST

***Dear Dragon Eats Out* uses the 68 words listed below.**

The **5** words bolded below serve as an introduction to new vocabulary, while the other 63 are pre-primer. You may wish to write the words on index cards and use them to help your child build automatic word recognition. Regular practice with these words will enhance your child's fluency in reading connected text.

a	for	let	**pancakes**	up
am	fun	let's	pick	
and		like	put	want
are	get	look		we
	go		ready	what
bacon	going	me		will
big	good	Mother	sit	with
boy			something	
but	have	need	spot	you
	help	no		
can	here	now	there	
come (s)	how		these	
		oh	things	
dear	I	ok	think	
do	I'll	on	this	
down	in	**orange**	to	
Dragon	is	out	today	
	it		too	
eat				
eggs	**juice**			

ABOUT THE AUTHOR Margaret Hillert has written over 80 books for children who are just learning to read. Her books have been translated into many different languages and over a million children throughout the world have read her books. She first started writing poetry as a child and has continued to write for children and adults throughout her life. A first grade teacher for 34 years, Margaret is now retired from teaching and lives in Michigan where she likes to write, take walks in the morning, and care for her three cats.

Photograph by Glenna Washburn

ABOUT THE ILLUSTRATOR David Schimmell served as a professional firefighter for 23 years before hanging up his boots and helmet to devote himself to working as an illustrator of children's books. David has happily created illustrations for the New Dear Dragon books as well as other artwork for educational and retail book projects. Born and raised in Evansville, Indiana, he lives there today with his wife and family.